THE GREATEST ADVENTURES IN THE WORLD

BEOWULF
THE
HERO

TONY BRADMAN & TONY ROSS

ORCHARD BOOKS

ORCHARD BOOKS
338 Euston Road, London NW1 3BH
Orchard Books Australia
Level 17/207 Kent Street, Sydney, NSW 2000
ISBN 978 1 40830 573 7 (hardback)
ISBN 978 1 40830 574 4 (paperback)
The text was first published in Great Britain in the form of a gift collection called
Heroes and Villains with full colour illustrations by Tony Ross, in 2008
This edition first published in hardback in 2010
First paperback publication in 2011
Text © Tony Bradman 2008
Illustrations © Tony Ross 2010
The rights of Tony Bradman to be identified as the author and of Tony Ross to be
identified as the illustrator of this work have been asserted by them in accordance
with the Copyright, Designs and Patents Act, 1988.
A CIP catalogue record for this book is available from the British Library.
1 3 5 7 9 10 8 6 4 2 (hardback)
1 3 5 7 9 10 8 6 4 2 (paperback)
Printed & bound in the UK by J F Print Ltd., Sparkford, Somerset.
Orchard Books is a division of Hachette Children's Books,
an Hachette UK company.
www.hachette.co.uk

CONTENTS

CHAPTER ONE

WARRIOR

LONG AGO, IN THE FAR-OFF DAYS of legend, when being a hero still counted for something in the cold, hard lands of the north, a young warrior called Beowulf heard a tale that set his mind racing with dreams of glory.

One night, a
monster called
Grendel had crept
into the hall of a
Danish chieftain by the
name of Rothgar.
The monster
killed many
of Rothgar's
warriors,
and left
nothing but their
blood splattered on
the walls. Grendel had
returned the next night, and every
night since.

So Rothgar had to leave his hall empty in the sunless hours, and his people lived in terror.

It was said that no one could stand up to Grendel and survive, although many mighty warriors had tried their hands against him. That made it even more tempting for Beowulf to take on the challenge himself. He was already known here and there in the north for his great strength.

But this was the perfect chance for him to show what he could really do.

"Imagine how famous I would be if I managed to kill the monster," he thought.

"It would be enough to make me a great hero…and harpists would sing about my exploits for thousands of years to come."

Beowulf soon set sail for Denmark, taking with him the band of young

warriors he often led into battle.
A week or so later, he and his
shield-brothers marched through
Rothgar's village, the northern sunlight
glinting on their helmets and mailshirts,
their sharp swords and spears.

Rothgar was sitting at the far end of his
hall, deep in moody thought, his face

clouded. A few of his warriors were
standing nearby. Beowulf strode up to him,
past heaps of smashed tables and benches,

all marked with gouges and scratches.
Bloodstains covered the walls, and
there was no bright, warming fire
burning in the dead hearth, only cold,
grey ashes.

"Hail, Rothgar," said Beowulf. "I've
come to solve your problem."

"Is that so?" said one of Rothgar's men,
looking Beowulf up and down. The man
obviously wasn't that impressed. "Well

then, who are you?"

"My name is Beowulf, a[n]
shield-brothers," the young wa[r]
returning the man's stare. "And wh[o]
might you be, friend?"

The man didn't bother to reply, but
turned to Rothgar instead. "Don't listen to
him, my lord," he said. "He can't help us.
He's like all the others. Full of boasting,
I'll bet, but no real match for a monster
like Grendel."

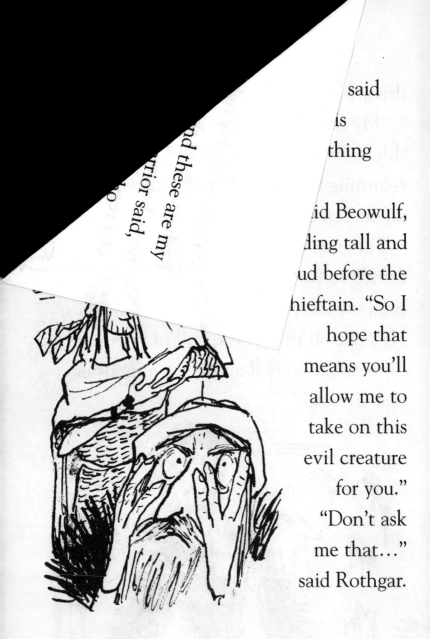

...said

...is

...thing

...id Beowulf, ...ding tall and ...ud before the ...hieftain. "So I hope that means you'll allow me to take on this evil creature for you."

"Don't ask me that..." said Rothgar.

...d these are my ...rior said,

"I would hate to see yet another young warrior slaughtered. What do you know about Grendel, anyway?"

"Not much," said Beowulf, shrugging. "Except that he haunts your hall at night, and has killed a lot of warriors. What else is there to know?"

"A great deal," said Unferth. "Grendel is strong and cunning and shows no mercy. When he chooses, he is harder to see than the shadow of a shadow. He finds ways in, where no creature of daylight could go…"

"And it also seems that no blade made by humans can harm him, nor even make a mark on his scaly hide," Rothgar muttered. "Some believe that he lives in a lake in the marshes with his mother, another creature of darkness and pure evil. So, young man – what do you say now?"

Beowulf hesitated. The truth was that he had begun to feel nervous. He hadn't fully understood just what a challenge Grendel might be till then – a straight fight was one thing, but grappling with the monster they had just described...well, that was different. But Beowulf kept an iron grip on himself, determined not to show what he was feeling inside. He hadn't come all this way only to give up at the first touch of fear.

"Exactly the same," he replied. "I'm here to rid you of this evil, and in front of every man present I swear that's what I will do. Or die trying."

Rothgar smiled, and his men seemed impressed – even Unferth.

"Very well," said Rothgar. "Tonight you will face the monster as you wish. And if you defeat him, I will reward you handsomely. But first let me feed you and your men. We still know how to treat guests here."

CHAPTER TWO

TERROR IN THE NIGHT

ROTHGAR TOLD HIS MEN TO clear up the hall as best they could, and get a fire going, and before long a marvellous feast was laid on for Beowulf and his men. Rothgar's wife came to meet

them, and laughter echoed in the rafters, something that hadn't been heard there for a very long time. But through the open doorway, Beowulf could see the daylight fading. Night was coming, and

he knew Grendel wouldn't be far behind.

Soon the feast was over, and the
moment came for Rothgar and his wife
and men to leave the hall. Rothgar wished
Beowulf luck. He gripped his hand and

19

talked of the gold and jewels and fine
weapons and horses he would give
him – if the young warrior survived the
night. But Beowulf could see in Rothgar's
sad eyes that the chieftain didn't think
he would…

"I won't be needing this," Beowulf said, giving his sword to one of his shield-brothers for safekeeping. He positioned them round the hall, and took a spot right in the middle, by the fire. He ordered his men to tell him as soon as they heard or saw anything, and then he  would step forward to fight Grendel with his bare hands. That was the plan, at any rate.

21

He had done plenty of wrestling in his time, and had beaten many strong men.

They settled down to wait, the darkness in the doorway deepening. Beowulf sat by the flickering firelight, the flamesshrinking, the shadows in the corners  of the hall lengthening and flowing into each other. One by one, Beowulf's men fell asleep, their chins nodding onto their chests. But Beowulf stayed awake.

Then his eyelids began to grow heavy too.

All at once the monster Grendel exploded out of the darkness, hissing and spitting and slashing at Beowulf with his sharp, curved talons.

The young warrior was knocked off his feet, crashing into the hearth and sending a shower of sparks flying, although he still managed to hold back the monster. Beowulf was on his back now with Grendel on top of him, the monster snarling and snapping and trying to rip out his throat.

Grendel stank of the marshes, and was slimy to the touch. He was incredibly strong too, exactly as Unferth had said. He pressed down on Beowulf, his foul breath beating into the young warrior's face, drool dripping from his pointed, yellow fangs.

Beowulf resisted with all his might,
and slowly began to force Grendel back.
He heard his shield-brothers shouting,
and suddenly a torch flared into life,
then another.

Beowulf could see his opponent now, the
thick, scaly, grey hide, the body like a

man's, although much bigger and rippling with muscle. The young warrior rolled to one side, holding the monster's wrists and trying to get on top of him. Soon they were on their knees, then on their feet, neither of them willing to let go, the terrible struggle continuing.

Monster and man stared at each other, their faces almost touching. Beowulf's men hacked at Grendel with their swords, but he seemed not to notice. He started

pressing Beowulf down once more,
torchlight glinting in his
black eyes. His mouth
widened in a
wicked smile,
and those
yellow fangs
came closer
and closer
to the soft
flesh of
Beowulf's
throat…

Beowulf
summoned up
all his massive
strength.

He squeezed the monster's wrists and pushed back at him again – and gradually he began to win. "You've met your match at last, Grendel." he muttered from between gritted teeth, and the monster's smile faded. Soon Beowulf could see fear in the monster's eyes, and feel him trying to pull away.

Eventually Beowulf pinned Grendel down, and secured both of the monster's wrists in one mighty hand. Then with the other he reached for Grendel's throat. Strangling would probably be the best way to kill him.

Grendel squealed in panic, freed one arm and desperately tried to escape.

Beowulf held on grimly, and warrior and monster crashed round the hall, smashing into the walls and knocking over Beowulf's men like so many skittles.

At last there was a great sound of flesh tearing and bones cracking, and the monster fled, howling, into the night, leaving Beowulf holding a strange and grisly trophy – Grendel's other arm and shoulder.

Beowulf nailed it to a beam, and his men cheered him to the rafters.

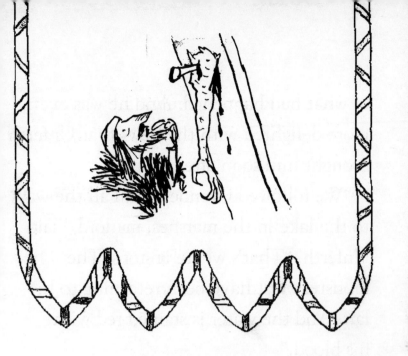

CHAPTER THREE

VICTORY!

IN THE MORNING, WHEN ROTHGAR
returned to his hall, he was amazed to see
Grendel's arm.

Of course he was also delighted that
Beowulf had lived to tell the incredible tale

of what had happened. And he was even more delighted with the news that Unferth brought him soon after.

"We followed Grendel's trail all the way to the lake in the marshes, my lord," said Unferth. "That's where it stops. The monster must have been returning to his lair. And the water is stained red with his blood."

"He couldn't possibly have survived such a wound…" said Rothgar. "Which means, Beowulf, that you are the greatest hero of our time!"

The young warrior grinned as everyone cheered again.

Then Rothgar laid on an even more magnificent feast, and brought out wonderful gifts for Beowulf and his men – all the fine things he had talked of, and lots more besides. Beowulf ate and drank and listened to the harpist singing, hardly able to believe that his exploits were the subject of the song.

That night, as he finally lay down to rest in Rothgar's hall along with everyone else, he felt utterly exhausted. He was bruised and battered too, and he knew that it had been a desperately close-run contest. The monster had tested him to the very limits of his strength.

Another moment or two and one of his arms might have been ripped out, not Grendel's.

"Well, thank goodness it's all over, anyway," thought Beowulf. He smiled as he remembered what Rothgar had said, and fell asleep…

But it wasn't over.
He woke to the sound
of screaming. People
were running round in
terror, their shadows
dancing in the firelight.

A huge shape
snarled and slashed at anyone who was
near, and finally vanished.

Torches flared, and Beowulf heard
gasps, followed by howls of grief.

He quickly pushed through the crowd
and saw Rothgar by a pool of blood.

A trail of red footprints led from the
blood to the hall door. And Grendel's arm
had gone, pulled down from the wall and
carried off into the night.

"Grim news, Beowulf," said Rothgar, turning to him. "Death still stalks my hall. I've lost another brave warrior to a monster from the marsh."

"What, you mean that Grendel isn't dead?" said Beowulf.

"Oh, Grendel is dead, right enough," Rothgar muttered, his face grim. "The beast who came here tonight had both her arms… I had always thought the story about Grendel having a mother was a tale to frighten little children. But it's true, and she came to seek revenge for her son."

CHAPTER FOUR

A MOTHER'S REVENGE

EVERYBODY IN THE HALL
started talking at once, their fear and
horror making them loud. Before long
they convinced themselves that Grendel's
mother was impossibly strong and far more

powerful than her son, and that she would return to hunt them each night, just as he had done.

"What shall we do?" somebody wailed at last. "We're all doomed!"

"Oh no we're not!" somebody else yelled. "Beowulf will save us!"

"Yes, Beowulf!" the crowd yelled. They turned to the young warrior, and they started to chant his name. "Beowulf! BEOWULF! BEOWULF!"

"ENOUGH!" Rothgar shouted at last, and the hall fell silent. "No man should be forced to fight such a hellish creature," said Rothgar. "And if you choose not to, Beowulf, you can still leave here with the gifts I gave you, and feel no shame. You've done your share, and I thank you."

All eyes were on the young warrior now. Beowulf was silent, deep in thought, his head down. Then he looked up at Rothgar, and at Unferth.

"And what if there is another monster, after I kill this one?" he said.

"Beowulf, there is always another monster," Rothgar said. "Or armies of invaders like hungry wolves in the winter, or other threats…"

And that's when Beowulf realised there was a lot more to this business of being a hero than he had thought. It seemed it wasn't just about glory, and harpists singing songs about your exploits. These people were relying on him. They had seen him take on one monster and win, and now they were expecting him to defeat a bigger, stronger, scarier opponent.

But what if he couldn't do it? Beowulf scanned the ring of faces before him, saw the hope and trust in their eyes – the belief that he would succeed again and save them. Suddenly all the fear inside him fell away. He knew he couldn't let these people down, even if it meant losing his life.

"So be it," he said, standing tall and proud. "I choose… to fight!"

A great roar went up in the hall, and soon Beowulf and his shield-brothers were on the trail of Grendel's mother.

Her huge footprints were plain to see beside the blood trail left by Grendel.

Rothgar had promised Beowulf more fine gifts, but the only thing on Beowulf's mind was killing the monster. He didn't care any more if harpists sang about him afterwards.

They did, though. They sang of how Beowulf found a mist-covered lake in the marshes, of how he plunged deep beneath its tainted surface and tracked Grendel's mother to her cave, of how he fought a mighty fight with her over the body of her dead son – and of how he won. They sang of how he returned with the heads of both monsters, and left Rothgar and his people free forever from the terror that had haunted their nights.

And we still sing the same song today – that of Beowulf the hero!

BEOWULF

One Man Against the Monsters

By Tony Bradman

Nobody knows whether one man or many created the story of Beowulf. We don't know when it was first told – some people think that might have been in the 8th century AD, others in 1000 AD or later. And we nearly didn't have it at all – the only manuscript was almost burnt in a fire in the 16th century.

We do know that it was originally a poem in Old English, the language of the Anglo-Saxons who invaded Britain and settled here after the Romans left. We also know that some of the people in the poem actually existed – Rothgar was a real king, and archaeologists have excavated his great hall in Denmark.

Like the Vikings, who invaded Britain later on, the Anglo-Saxons were a warrior people. Their Gods were fierce and demanded the sacrifice of animals, and sometimes even human beings. The Anglo-Saxons loved to hear stories of men fighting and courage in war, and also of strange, mythical monsters.

All these things came together in the story of Beowulf. Perhaps he did exist, and did travel to help Rothgar. And perhaps a tale of his adventures was passed from person to person, then made into a poem to be told on winter evenings in the hall of a great lord, his people feasting around him, the hearth fire flickering.

It's not surprising that a magical thread was woven into the story – what is more natural in the tale of a legendary hero than an encounter with a mythical monster? Beowulf's battle with Grendel is a lot like the tales of Greek heroes such as Theseus and the Minotaur, and Perseus killing the Gorgon, Medusa.

But there was something about the character of Beowulf that has made people want to read his story over and over again, or make it into longer stories and even films. That something is the way in which Beowulf shows true courage. He kills one monster – but then he has to fight a far worse one, Grendel's mother. Beowulf shows us that one person can face many problems – and survive.

ORCHARD MYTHS AND CLASSICS

THE GREATEST ADVENTURES IN THE WORLD

TONY BRADMAN & TONY ROSS

All priced at £8.99

Orchard books are available from all good bookshops,
or can be ordered from our website: www.orchardbooks.co.uk,
or telephone 01235 827702, or fax 01235 827703

Prices and availability are subject to change.